The Old Woman
& the Wave

The Old Woman & the Wave

SHELLEY JACKSON

A DK INK BOOK
DK PUBLISHING, INC.

For Awesome, a gentle soul.

A Richard Jackson Book

DK Publishing, Inc.
95 Madison Avenue
New York, New York 10016
Visit us on the World Wide Web at http://www.dk.com
Copyright © 1998 by Shelley Jackson

Library of Congress Cataloging-in-Publication Data
Jackson, Shelley.
The old woman and the wave / written and illustrated by Shelley
Jackson. — 1st ed.
p.   cm.
Summary: An old woman finally comes to understand and appreciate
the huge wave that has hung in the air, sheltering her house,
all her life.
ISBN 0-7894-2484-3
[1. Water — Fiction.]   I. Title.
PZ7.J137501 1997 [E] — dc21 97-34114 CIP AC

The text of this book is set in 18 point Cochin.
Printed and bound in U.S.A.
First Edition, 1998
2 4 6 8 10 9 7 5 3 1

Once upon a time there was an old woman who
lived under a wave. The wave never fell, but
there was always the chance that it might, so every
day the old woman went to the door of her
cottage and looked out.

"Still there, wave?" she bellowed.

How could she know that the wave bent low when she yelled, just to hear her? The wave loved the old woman. But because the old woman had lived her whole life beneath it, she could see nothing good in the wave. She squinted for fear of a drop in the eye and hunched for fear of a drip down her collar. She never noticed the wave stretch its glassy body against the sun so the light was a blue-green shout in its stomach. She never saw the swallows wet their claws in the top of the wave and dare one another to fly under the tangled crest.

"How you can stand to live under that wave I'll never know," said the old man from down the road.

"Drip-drop," said the old woman. "I was born here and I'll die here."

In case the wave ever fell, the woman had built a little boat out of a washtub, a table leg, and an old apron. It had a cracked shovel for a rudder and an old broom for an oar. She kept it locked in a shed, and the key swung around her neck day and night.

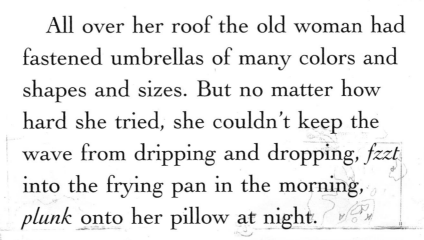

All over her roof the old woman had fastened umbrellas of many colors and shapes and sizes. But no matter how hard she tried, she couldn't keep the wave from dripping and dropping, *fzzt* into the frying pan in the morning, *plunk* onto her pillow at night.

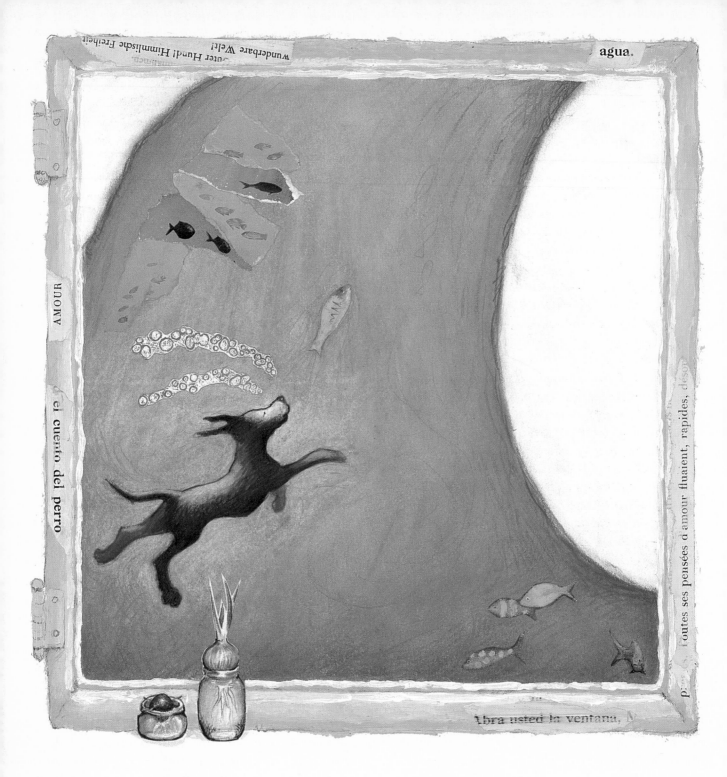

To make matters worse, old Bones, her dog,
loved the wave. Sometimes she looked out of
the cottage to see Bones, bubbles streaming from
his muzzle, chasing fish in the belly of the wave.
"Drip-drop," she said. "Shows how much sense
you have."

Often he slunk home wet from teeth to toenails. "Wicked Bones! Wicked wave!" she scolded.

A fish leaped from the wave and landed at her feet.

She picked it up and threw it back at the wave, which swallowed it. "Wasteful!" she roared. "Don't bother trying to soften me up!" And she slammed the door.

In the morning the light ran in liquid patterns across the walls of the old woman's cottage, and shadows of fish swam in at her window and across her blanket, waking her up. But the old woman just grumbled and turned her face to the wall. "I'll get up when I get up," she muttered. Yet a minute later her feet swung out of the covers and hunted for her slippers under the bed.

The old woman stepped out the door. "Still there, wave?" she yelled. The wave stood tall and shook itself, spattering her with drops. "Careless!" she said.

A fish leaped from the wave and landed wiggling in the grass at her feet. "Clumsy!" scolded the old woman, popping the fish in her apron to fry with butter and thyme for lunch.

She was picking pebbles out of the flower beds
and tossing them back on the garden path when
a wanderer rapped at the gate.

The stranger was young and strong and looking
for work to do, so the old woman fed her on
fish and sent her up to the roof to patch the
umbrellas.

When she was done, the stranger sat on the chimney swinging her legs and looking up at the wave. She was whistling a strange little tune that made the old woman think of a bird flying in and out of a waterfall.

"Don't waste your time on that wave," the old woman called up sharply.

"That wave could take someone a long way, if someone wanted to go," said the wanderer, hopping off the chimney.

"You're welcome to it," said the old woman. "Take it with you when you go."

"I'd like to," said the wanderer wistfully as she climbed down the ladder. "But it's not the wave for me." She settled her hat and marched off down the gravel path.

The old woman rushed to the gate to look after her. "But where are you going?" she cried, for she had lived alone in the one house all her days.

"Away," said the wanderer, without looking back. "I just want to see . . ." She pointed down the road toward the blue and distant mountains, and, strangely, the old woman knew just what she meant. The old woman had never seen the mountains or the sea. She hobbled after her, but the stones hurt her bunions and the wanderer was already far ahead, and at last the old woman turned back.

"Drip-drop, at least I've got my Bones," she sighed, and cast her eye about. "Bones," she called. "Bones?" She whistled and clapped. "Bones!"

A smart smack of water landed on her forehead, firm as a kiss. "Why, you—" she said, and looked up, and then farther up, and farther still.

Bones?

mein Hund!

perro?

chien?

hond

BONES

BONES!

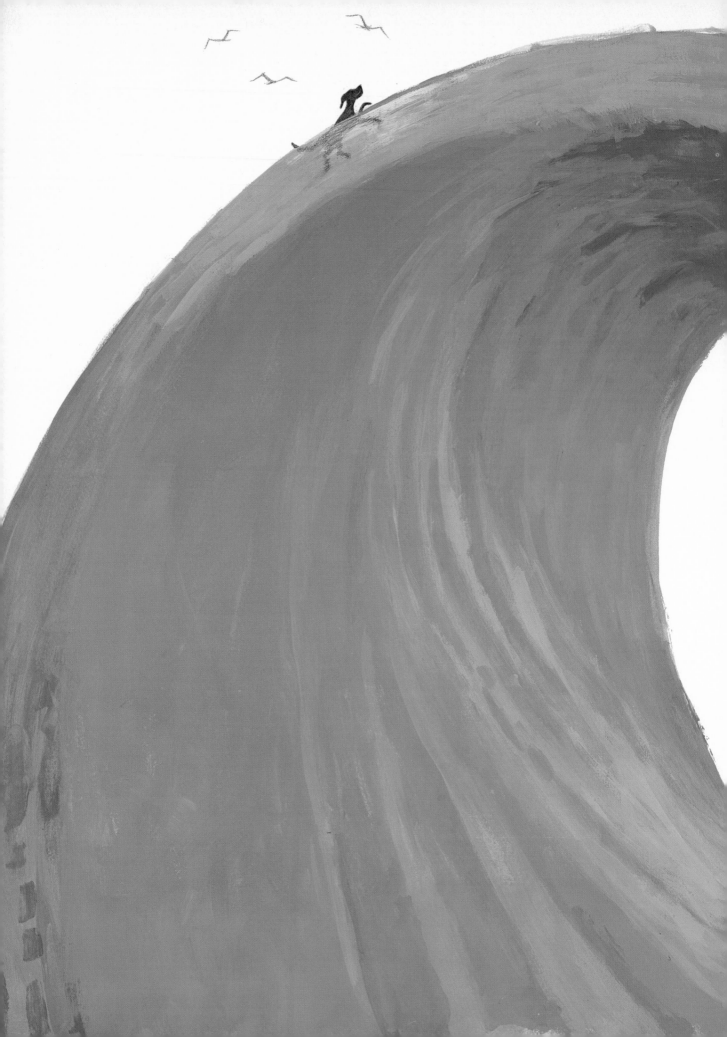

There was Bones, swimming high. He was up where the sun rode, up where the swallows fooled around in the spray.

"For shame!" she scolded the wave. But the wave stood like a statue as tall as the sky, Bones near the top of it. "Give me back my Bones," she roared to the wave, "or I'll tell the sun to dry you up, drip-drop!"

The old woman hurried to the shed with her little key and dragged out the boat. "I'll fetch that dog home," she muttered. She turned the boat over on her head and scurried to where the grass was always wet. There she set the boat against the side of the wave.

She rowed

and heaved

and strained up the wave
till her shoulders ached
and sweat ran off her arms.

At last, far ahead, she saw old Bones's
ears against the sky.

"Bones!" she shouted. The dog swam
back toward her, looking smug, but
he let the old woman help him into the
boat. "Where did you think you were
off to?"

Bones wagged his wet tail.

The old woman wiped her face. She and the dog
rested at the top of the wave, which murmured
and sighed underneath them. The sun soothed her
tired shoulders. Lights danced on the wave
around her. The blue sky was close enough to
touch, and the mountains just a splash and a
plunge away.

She looked down at the house stuck all over with umbrellas. Suddenly the old woman laughed. "What a silly thing I am!" Bones wagged his tail again — *boom, boom, boom* — on the side of the washtub.

"Wave," the old woman said
finally, pleased with herself. "I see,
I see. But slowly, now!" The wave
shimmered and a ripple went
through it.

Then the wave lay down on
the land.

Everything began to ripple and flow. The wave
became a river, surging and plunging, swirling
and curling, and flowing away, away, but never
upsetting the boat in which Bones and the old
woman rode.

Running after, the man from down the road
cried, "But where are you going?"

"Away!" shouted the old woman. She didn't look
back. She looked straight ahead at the mountains,
and the waves that carried her toward them.